Meet at
the Ark at
Eight!

Meet at the Ark at Eight!

Ulrich Hub

Illustrated by Jörg Mühle

PUSHKIN CHILDREN'S BOOKS

Pushkin Children's Books
71–75 Shelton Street,
London WC2H 9JQ

Originally published as *An der Arche um Acht*
© S. Fischer Verlag GmbH, Frankfurt am Main, 2014

First published by Patmos Verlag GmbH & Co.KG,
Sauerländer Verlag, Düsseldorf, 2007

English language translation © Helena Ragg-Kirkby, 2012

0 0 1

ISBN 978 1 782690 87 0

Typeset by Tetragon, London
Printed and bound by CPI Group (UK) Ltd, Croydon CRO 4YY

www.pushkinchildrens.com

Somewhere in the world is a place made of ice and snow. Wherever you look, you see only snow and ice and ice and snow and snow and ice.

If you look more closely, you can see three small figures in the snow and ice. They are standing close together, looking around. Wherever they look, they too can see nothing but ice and snow and snow and ice and ice and snow.

If you get closer to these three figures, you can tell that they are three penguins. They all look the same. But that's the way it is. All penguins look the same. If you've seen one, you've seen them all.

Get even closer to these three penguins, though, and you can definitely see that one of them is different. He's a bit smaller than the other two. But beware! No one should get too close to penguins. They might be completely harmless, but they have a distinctly fishy smell.

"You stink," says the first penguin.

"So do you," replies the second.

"Oh, stop bickering," says the little one, giving the other two a kick.

If you kick a penguin, he will always kick you back, probably a bit harder. One kick follows another, then a full-scale brawl quickly ensues until all the penguins suddenly flop down in the snow and look at each other in complete bafflement. "Why on earth are we always fighting?"

Every day is the same. First the penguins look around, then they look at one another, and then they start fighting. "If only something would happen for a change," sighs the little penguin.

On this particular day, something does happen. Something unusual. The unusual thing is small and yellow. It flutters three times around the penguins' heads and then lands in the snow.

"A butterfly!" The penguins leap for joy, clapping their wings excitedly. Only much later will they realize that the appearance of the butterfly means the start of a huge catastrophe. The penguins waddle cautiously over to the butterfly and gaze at it, enchanted. They have never seen anything so beautiful.

"I'm going to do him in right now," says the little penguin.

"Leave the butterfly alone!" the other two cry.

"But I want to do him in," pleads the little one.

"Thou shalt not kill."

"Who says so?"

"God," the other two penguins reply. "God said, 'Thou shalt not kill'!"

"Oh," the little one says. He pauses for a moment, then asks, "So who is God?"

If you ask a penguin who God is, he never knows quite how to answer. "Oh, God… that's a difficult question," the first penguin stammers. "Well, God is great and very, very powerful. He came up with all kinds of rules and can become quite grumpy if you don't stick to them. Other than that, he's very friendly."

"There's just one small disadvantage to God," the second penguin adds.

"What's that?" the little one asks, intrigued.

"God is invisible."

"Well, that's a huge disadvantage," the little penguin says, looking disappointed. "If you can't see God, you can't be sure whether he really exists."

The other two penguins look at one another helplessly. Then they ask the little one, "Look around you and describe what you see."

"Snow," the little penguin says. He doesn't look around, since he already knows the answer.

"What else?"

"Ice."

"What else?"

"Snow."

"What else?!"

"Ice and snow and snow and ice and ice —"

"And who made it all?"

"God?" says the little penguin doubtfully.

"Precisely." The other two nod vigorously. "So what do you have to say about that?"

"I'd say he was a bit short on inspiration when he made this place."

The other two penguins flinch and look up at the sky nervously. "Be quiet — he might hear you," they whisper.

8

"God has incredibly good hearing and, what's more, he made us penguins."

"In that case, he must have got confused somehow," the little penguin retorts. "We're birds, but we smell like fish; we have wings, but we can't fly."

"But we can swim!"

True. Penguins are, in fact, excellent swimmers. But it's hard to discuss things with penguins. Once they have an idea in their heads, it's impossible to convince them otherwise.

"Anyway," the little penguin says stubbornly, "God made more of an effort with this butterfly, because it can use its wings to fly wherever it likes. That's not fair, and that's why I'm going to do it in right now."

"If you do, you'll be punished," the other two warn him.

"By whom?"

"By God!"

"Well, I can't wait," the little penguin giggles, raising his foot so he can stomp on the butterfly.

That would have been the end of the butterfly, but something stops the little penguin — a smack on both ears. He looks bewildered, then starts to wail.

"Yes, cry all you like," say the others, unmoved. "You behave badly, you have to be told everything three times, and you're altogether a very bad penguin."

No penguin enjoys being told that he is a bad penguin. But the little one acts as though he doesn't care. Defiantly, he flops down onto the snow. "So what? There are good penguins and bad ones; I'm one of the bad ones. That's the way I've always been. I can't do anything about it. In any case, it's not my fault. That's just the way God made me."

Horrified, the other two penguins flap their wings in front of his face. "You just sat on the butterfly!"

The little penguin jumps up quickly and looks around. The butterfly is lying in the snow right where he has been sitting. It is still small and yellow, but it is no longer fluttering. Its left wing is completely crushed.

Together, the three penguins bend down over the butterfly.

"The poor thing is dead," the first one says.

The second one adds: "He'll go to heaven now."

"Does everyone who dies go to heaven?" the little penguin asks.

"No, not everyone. Only good people go to heaven. So you won't."

"I'm not good?" the little one asks, baffled.

The other two shake their heads. "You just killed a butterfly."

"But I didn't mean to!"

"You said you wanted to do him in, and now he's dead." They point to the butterfly, lying motionless in the snow. "God won't be very pleased with that."

"Maybe God wasn't looking," the little penguin murmurs.

"God has incredibly good eyesight. He can see every-

thing, and when you die and think you can just stroll into heaven, he'll be there in person at the gates, waiting to have a word with you."

"By then," says the little one, trying to hide the slight tremble in his voice, "he'll have long since forgotten about the butterfly."

"I wouldn't bet your life on it. God has a superb memory and he never forgets to punish a penguin who hasn't stuck to the rules."

"What kind of punishment?"

"You just wait and see." The other two penguins exchange looks, grinning. "God might have been short on inspiration when he created this place, but he's full of ideas when it comes to inventing punishments."

"I don't believe in God." The little penguin stamps his foot. "You've just made him up to scare me. I don't need any

God. I've got along fine without him up until now. And as for you two" — the little penguin has tears in his eyes by this point — "I don't need you either. I don't want friends who scare me. I never want to see you again!"

Then he waddles off so quickly that snow flies up in clouds behind him.

Perplexed, the other two penguins watch him go.

"What's got into him all of a sudden?" asks the first penguin.

"Maybe he's right," replies the second penguin. "I've never seen God, and I don't know anyone who has. God ought to show himself occasionally."

"Shh." The first penguin lowers his voice. "God's watching us. Even now — can't you feel it? Just look at the sky."

Both penguins tilt their heads back and look up. They see dark, heavy clouds. The first penguin points his wing at the sky and says solemnly, "God is marching up and down behind those clouds, watching us closely."

"Nonsense," the second penguin replies. "God can't see us at all. The black clouds stop him from seeing when he's marching around on the edge of the sky."

At that very moment a large white dove comes fluttering through the air, steers toward them, and lands clumsily in the snow, doing several somersaults in the process.

The two penguins watch this landing manoeuvre with much fascination. *Well, we can't complain about being bored today*, they think. *First the little butterfly, and now a dove.*

The dove, meanwhile, has recovered. She staggers up, shakes the snow from her wings, and stands before the two penguins, her legs apart. "Do you have a minute?" she asks. She continues before they have a chance to say anything. "Okay then. I'm bringing you a message from God. Listen closely. God says — But what's that fishy smell?"

"That's us," the two penguins reply. Intrigued, they waddle closer to the dove.

"Then don't get so close to me, for God's sake!" the dove screeches, leaping backward. "God's had enough of humans and animals. They never stop arguing, and you have to say everything to them three times. God's finally lost patience with them. That's what he said." The dove pauses for effect before continuing in a lowered voice, "God said, 'I'm going to send a great flood. The seas and rivers will rise higher and higher until they wash over the shores and everything vanishes under water. The water will rise above the houses, above the treetops, and even above the top of the highest mountain. Eventually the whole planet will be flooded with water. And that'll be that.'" The dove takes a deep breath and then drops down onto the snow, exhausted. "Now I've told all the animals in the world. You two were the last."

The two penguins listen, open-beaked. "But that means the end of the world!"

"That's precisely God's plan." The dove pulls a little bottle from her bag, unscrews the top, and takes a long swig. "God wants to wipe out the whole world and start again from scratch. And you two," she adds, giving them a stern look, "really do stink."

"But what's going to happen to all the humans and animals?" the penguins ask, their voices trembling.

The dove doesn't reply. She carefully screws the cap back on her bottle. Finally, she shrugs and says, "They'll find out soon enough."

"Find out what?"

"Well…"

"That they're all going to drown?"

"You said it." The dove gives the two penguins a reproachful look.

The first penguin turns toward the second one. "You always wanted God to show himself," he says. "Well, you got what you wanted. I don't think he can show himself any more clearly than that."

"But does it have to be a full-scale flood?" the second penguin asks the dove despairingly. "Can't someone have another chat with God and get him to change his mind?"

The dove tilts her head to one side. "I don't know God personally, but it's hard to discuss things with him. Once he has an idea in his head, it's impossible to convince him otherwise. In any case, it's too late. It's already starting to rain."

Indeed it is. The two penguins look upward. Fat raindrops are already splashing down onto their heads.

"Stop, please stop," the two penguins whimper, reaching their wings out pleadingly to the sky. "We promise we'll never quarrel again. We'll be good for ever and ever."

"Stop wailing," the dove says firmly, "and start packing."

"Packing?"

"There's space in Noah's ark for two penguins — didn't I mention that?" asks the dove. She continues without waiting for an answer. "We're taking two of each species on board. We need two elephants, two weasels, two hedgehogs, two zebras,

two kangaroos, two raccoons, two snakes, two deer, two squirrels, two giraffes, two sparrows, two lions, two dogs, two crocodiles, two geese, two camels, two cats, two ants —"

The penguins' heads are starting to spin. "But why just two?"

"Noah's ark is enormous," the dove replies impatiently, "but it doesn't have unlimited space. So only two of each species is allowed on board. Here are the tickets. Don't lose them!"

On the front of the tickets is a picture of a big ship sailing across a blue sea. On the back it says in small print:

This ticket is valid for passage only, and does not entitle the holder to a seat. Tickets are non-refundable, and will become invalid after the flood.

Neither penguin has any objections. But reading is in any case not a penguin's strong point.

"Remember," the dove warns them, "you have to meet at the ark at eight o'clock. If you're late, you'll drown."

Before the dove rises into the air, she looks at the two penguins and says, "Hmm. I have a funny feeling that I've forgotten something. Something important." She scratches her head and mutters, "It'll come back to me."

Then the plump dove flaps her wings, rises into the air with considerable difficulty, and flutters away through the rain.

The two penguins start packing feverishly. But their minds aren't entirely on the job. The first one is thinking, *We were chosen because we are the best penguins of all. Especially me. We have always been good. Especially me. That's why we have tickets for Noah's ark. Otherwise we'd drown, like —* he pauses.

Meanwhile, the second penguin is thinking,

Well, we were lucky. If we hadn't bumped into that dove, we'd be drowning now. Life is so strange. If two other penguins had been standing here, they'd have been given these tickets, and we'd have ended up drowning miserably, like — The penguin suddenly stops packing. A terrible thought has crossed his mind. "What's going to happen to our friend now?" he says aloud.

There is no reply. Both penguins stare at the rain, watching as the water rises higher and higher. Finally the first penguin shrugs and says: "He'll notice sooner or later."

"What?"

"Well —"

"That he's drowning?"

"You said it," he replies, looking reproachful.

"Are you planning to sit there calmly and watch our friend drown?"

"No, I'm not going to watch. I'm going to be miles away on Noah's ark when he drowns. Don't give me that funny look: the flood wasn't my idea!" And without having put anything into his suitcase, he slams the top shut and says, "For goodness' sake, just start packing."

The second penguin stares into his suitcase, wondering what he will need most on an ark. "We should pack our little penguin and smuggle him on board."

"Are you crazy? If anyone finds out, they'll send us flying — and then no penguins will survive." As he speaks, his voice toots like a little trumpet. "The survival of the whole penguin species depends on us. Do you hear?"

The business about the survival of the species does make sense to the second penguin. Gloomily, he shuts the lid of his empty suitcase and murmurs, "I would at least like to see him one last time."

"Fine by me," mumbles the first penguin. "But he won't be pleased to see us. If I know him, he'll still be in a huff."

But the little penguin isn't in a huff. Instead, he is standing under an umbrella thinking, *Why on earth did I say I could do without my friends? Now I've got nobody to quarrel with. If only I could*

waddle back to them and say I made a mistake. That, however, would be impossible. No penguin likes to admit that he has made a mistake. "I'll have to spend the rest of my life on my own," the little penguin thinks, staring at his tiny feet. They are slowly being covered by the rising water.

Suddenly he hears two familiar voices. "We just happened to be passing, and thought we'd stop by."

The little penguin looks up. In front of him are the other two penguins. They are both carrying suitcases.

"Are you going away?"

"What gives you that idea?" The other two laugh awkwardly and try to hide their suitcases behind their backs. They say no more, but look at the little penguin with big eyes and sigh.

"It's raining," says the little penguin.

"Oh," the other two say. "We hadn't noticed." They look up at the sky. The rain is coming down in torrents.

"It looks to me," says the little one, "as if the rain is never going to stop."

"Oh, it will stop," the other two say quickly, looking at their submerged feet. After this they fall silent again.

"You'd better come under my umbrella, or you'll catch a cold."

The other two penguins don't stir.

"If three penguins are standing in the rain," the little one goes on cheerfully, "and only one of them has an umbrella, then of course he asks his friends to come under it."

"You put it so beautifully," the other two say quietly, looking at him with damp eyes.

"Are those tears in your eyes?"

"They're raindrops." Quickly, they turn away and heave an enormous sigh.

The little penguin finds these sighs and tears strange. He is about to say something along those lines, but doesn't get the chance, because the other two penguins have started behaving even more strangely. They curl up their wings into little fists and give the little penguin such a hard blow on the head that he sees stars. Then he loses consciousness and sees nothing more. And thus he doesn't know that the other two have grabbed hold of him and are trying to stuff him into a suitcase.

Although the little penguin isn't particularly big, he doesn't fit into either suitcase.

It takes the other two penguins a long time to find a larger suitcase. Then they have to cram the little one inside, shut the lid, and secure it with two buckles, one of which is distinctly stiff. And so by the time the two penguins arrive at the ark carrying the big, heavy suitcase, it is already dark.

The dove is standing at the entrance to the ark in the pouring rain, bellowing hoarsely. "Last call for passengers! We urgently ask the two penguins to make their way to Noah's ark. Last call for all passengers!"

When she sees the two penguins wading through the knee-high water, carrying a big suitcase above their heads, she snaps at them, "Where on earth have you been? You're the last two! All the other animals have been on board for ages. Even the tortoises were quicker than you. Noah was all ready to go without you. I told you to be at the ark at eight o'clock!"

"Ah," the two penguins say, dragging the suitcase up to the gangway steps. "We thought you said to be at the ark at midnight."

The dove stares at the suitcase.

"I hope you're not planning to bring that on board. I said hand luggage only."

"We can't possibly leave this suitcase behind."

"Why not?"

The penguins mumble a bit and shuffle their feet.

"What's in this giant suitcase?" asks the dove.

"Just air."

"Why is it so heavy, then?"

"Because it's full of heavy air," say the two penguins, groaning under its weight.

The dove has strict instructions from Noah to open any questionable packages.

She bends down suspiciously over the suitcase and sniffs at it. "This suitcase smells like fish," she declares. "Are you trying to smuggle a fish sandwich on board or something?"

"It's us," the two penguins reply. "We always smell like fish."

"Passengers aren't allowed to bring their own food and drink," the dove continues, unperturbed. "We have a small concession stand on board. Open up that suitcase."

"It's completely harmless."

"I don't believe a word of it." The dove doesn't take her eyes off the suitcase.

"We're *penguins*," say the penguins with a nervous laugh. "You can trust us."

"That's what the rattlesnakes said." The dove gives an ironic laugh. "And what did I find in their hand luggage? A card game!"

"That's outrageous." The penguins are genuinely shocked.

"All forms of gambling," the dove continues, "are strictly prohibited on Noah's ark."

The first penguin assures her that there is definitely no card game in their suitcase. For once, he is telling the truth. The second penguin, meanwhile, is asking how snakes manage to play cards. But the dove says she has no desire to continue the conversation and that she is going to open the suitcase here and now. If, she says, there is anything inside it but fresh air, the penguins can forget about the ark and will just have to drown. And then there will be no more penguins ever again — which, she adds, is a matter of complete indifference to her.

The two penguins look at one another, take a deep breath, and stammer, "Okay then. In the suitcase… we just couldn't bring ourselves to… but it's really only a very small one…"

At that moment there is a flash of lightning that bathes everything in a lurid glow. It is followed by thunder so loud that it echoes around the world. Now the storm has really started. Buckets of water rain down from the sky.

"The flood!" shrieks the dove. "It's starting! Why are you

standing around chattering? Hurry up and get that suitcase on board, for goodness' sake — I've got to shut the doors!"

Gasping, the two penguins shove the heavy suitcase through the entrance to the ark.

Before the dove closes the door, she takes a last look at the earth, which will soon be completely under water. "Hmm. I have a funny feeling that I've forgotten something. Something important." She scratches her head and murmurs, "It'll come back to me." Then she quickly pulls the door shut behind her.

Anyone who has been on Noah's ark knows how enormous it is. It is three stories high, and so big that you can easily get lost on it. Noah is immensely proud of his ark, although he says that God did give him a few tips about building it. For example, he recommended that Noah make it out of pine and then paint it with tar to keep the water out.

The two penguins, however, have no opportunity to appreciate Noah's skill. Puffing and panting under the weight of the suitcase, they follow the dove as she shoos them down endless long corridors. They have to climb over ventilation pipes and down countless steep steps until they have completely lost their bearings. If one of them groans under the burden, the dove turns to them and hisses angrily, "Be quiet. The other animals have been asleep for ages."

At the end of a long passageway, the dove opens a door and disappears inside. It is pitch black. The two penguins stumble after her with their suitcase.

"Where are we?"

"You're right at the bottom," whispers the dove. "Down in the very bowels of the boat."

The two penguins put the suitcase down and look around them. It is dark, aside from a single lightbulb that dangles from the ceiling, casting its weak light on a couple of barrels. Everything is creaking and groaning.

"What's that funny smell?"

"That's tar," says the dove, pointing to the barrels. "Noah painted the ark with tar so that no water could get inside."

"Tar?!" the two penguins screech, horrified.

"Quiet, or you'll wake the other animals." The dove looks anxiously up at the ceiling. "Lions are particularly light sleepers."

"This stink is almost unbearable."

"Your fishy smell will soon drown it out," the dove says coolly. She turns to go. "Any other questions?"

Of course the penguins have questions. All kinds of questions! They want to know how long the buffet will be open; whether you have to change for dinner; where they can rent lounge chairs; whether there is a pool on deck; whether gymnastics are available on board, and —

"Where on earth do you think you are?" the dove yells, her face turning beetroot red. "This is a rescue operation, not a luxury cruise!"

Just then there is a loud roar from somewhere up above. The two penguins jump, and the dove looks at the ceiling

and rolls her eyes. "Look what you've done. Now the lions are awake again. It's not easy getting lions to sleep, especially when you're a dove. I'm going to leave now, but I don't want to hear another peep out of you."

"Hang on," say the penguins indignantly. "Are we supposed to spend the whole time down here?"

"You should consider yourselves lucky to have a place at all," the dove replies peevishly. "The ark is completely stuffed full of animals. Yes, it's dark down here and there's not much air, but at least you've got your own space. Upstairs, you can't move because of all the animals."

"But what are we supposed to do, stuck down here?"

"Sleep. Like the other animals."

"When will we get there?"

"We haven't even set off yet," screeches the dove at the top of her voice, "and you're asking when we'll get there?"

At that moment, an ear-splitting trumpeting sound comes from up above. The penguins jump, and the dove wails, "Oh, great! The elephants have woken up. It's all your —"

Suddenly there is a violent jolt. The bottom of the ship starts to sway. The dove clatters into the penguins. The suitcase starts to slide across the floor. Trembling, the birds cling to one another. Terrible screams come from all around them. Bears growling, sheep baaing, pigs grunting, elephants trumpeting, geese cackling, monkeys chattering, goats bleating, horses neighing, dogs barking, roosters crowing, frogs croaking, chickens clucking, owls screeching, snakes hissing, hippos belching, deer saying nothing, cows mooing, wolves howling, cats meowing — in short, a deafening noise.

Eventually the noise dies down. All that can be heard is a rhythmic splashing. The floor sways gently. The bulb that hangs down from the ceiling swings slowly back and forth, back and forth.

"We've cast off," says the dove. "Noah's ark is moving. Have a good journey."

In the doorway, the dove turns back and looks at the two penguins standing there trembling in the bowels of the ark, clutching one another with their wings.

"Hmm," she says. "I have a funny feeling that I've forgotten something. Something important." She scratches her head and murmurs, "It'll come back to me." Then she quickly shuts the door behind her.

The two penguins immediately open the suitcase. "I hope he hasn't suffocated in there."

The little penguin is squashed up inside the suitcase like an accordion. The other two prod him with their wings. He doesn't stir. They put their heads into the suitcase and sniff him. He smells distinctly strange.

The little penguin looks stone dead at first — but when he hears the first penguin saying, "I'm sure he'll go to heaven," he shoots out of the suitcase like a coiled spring, looks around, and asks excitedly, "Where am I?"

"On Noah's ark."

"What's that funny smell?"

"That's tar," the others explain. "But you get used to it."

33

"I don't like it here much," the little penguin says. "I'm going home."

The other two gently explain to him that home is gone and that God has covered the whole world with water.

The little penguin swallows hard. "So there really is a God?"

"He's proved it beyond all doubt," the other two say, grabbing him by the scruff of the neck. "You never stop creating difficulties. Only two penguins are allowed on board, but we smuggled you on. Nobody can ever find out — do you hear?"

"What about the other penguins?" asks the little penguin, but there is no reply. The other two are staring at their feet. They finally shrug and reply, "They'll notice sooner or later."

"What?"

"Well —"

"That they're drowning?!"

"You said it." The other two penguins look balefully at the little one.

"God's letting all the other animals drown?"

The other two try to explain that God is somehow unhappy and has sort of had enough of them all, so he wants to start again from scratch — though they have to admit that they haven't really grasped it themselves either.

"But I have," the little penguin says, slowly waddling over to the furthest corner and starting to sob quietly. "It's all my fault. I said there wasn't a God, and that's why he sent this flood."

"Oh, he didn't hear you."

"Yes he did," sobs the little penguin. "God has incredibly good hearing. I'm a bad penguin. I was even proud of it and, what's more" — his voice drops — "I killed someone."

"Who?"

"The butterfly."

"Oh, we'd long since forgotten about that."

"But God hasn't," the penguin says, starting to sob more loudly. "God has an incredibly good memory."

"God wasn't watching at all," the other two assure him. "He had his hands full, preparing for the flood. A flood isn't easy, even for someone like God. And in any case, you didn't intend to sit on the butterfly. It was an accident."

"I'm not so sure," the little penguin admits. "I wanted to sit down, and I thought, 'There's something yellow there.' Then I sat down, and thought, 'Was it the butterfly?' But then I thought, 'Whatever it was, I'm sitting down now, and if it was the butterfly, then that's just tough luck…'"

The little penguin is sobbing so bitterly by this point that his whole body is shaking. The other two dry his tears. "But the butterfly isn't dead," they assure him. "It came to pretty much right away — you'd have seen it for yourself if you

hadn't run off. It shook itself a bit and flew off. Its left wing was still a bit crushed, which made it rock a bit as it flew away, but —"

This isn't quite true, for neither of the penguins have given a second thought to the butterfly, but they have to make the little one quiet down at all costs. The entire ark can probably hear his wailing.

"You're only saying that to try to make me feel better." The little penguin pulls away from them, throws himself onto his stomach, and drums his wings against the floor. "I killed a butterfly and brought misery to the whole world!" He

reaches his wings up to the ceiling and shouts with all his might, "I believe in you, God! But why are you punishing everyone else? One little penguin offended you, but you're taking revenge on the whole world! Do you call that justice? I'm angry with you. Very, very angry. Do you hear me, God? Do you hear me?"

Whether or not God hears him, the dove certainly does. She rushes down to the bowels of the ark. At the very last moment, the first penguin jumps into the suitcase and pulls the lid shut — not a second too soon. The dove flings the door open. "Can't you behave like normal animals?" she screeches. "Everyone can hear you up on deck! You're supposed to be asleep!"

If the dove looked a bit more closely, she might notice that one of the penguins is a bit smaller than before. "I've got enough on my plate," she says. "The two antelopes don't want to sleep near the lions for some unfathomable reason. The two woodpeckers are making holes in the bottom of the boat. One ant has lost her partner and is looking for him everywhere. And Noah's not much use, either. He just keeps saying, 'Do this, do that, go on, get a move on!' And he hasn't even said 'thanks' yet, and —"

The dove suddenly stops and looks more closely at the two penguins. "That penguin looks different."

The little one is too scared to speak, but the second one says quickly, "All penguins look the same."

"That's what I'd always thought until now," says the dove, looking from one to the other. "But this penguin has shrunk."

"Penguins do shrink."

"Hmm," says the dove. She looks the little one straight in the eye. "Why isn't he saying anything?"

The little one clears his throat and croaks, "I'm hungry."

"His voice sounds different too."

"That's the hunger speaking," the two penguins say simultaneously, and start to tremble.

The dove takes a deep breath and rolls her eyes. Then, looking grumpy, she gives the penguins a packet of crackers. "That was supposed to be my food for the journey, so keep your beaks shut. We're not allowed to bring our own food on board, but the other animals aren't sticking to that either. The kangaroos even brought picnic baskets."

As the penguins pounce greedily on the crackers, the dove regrets her sudden rush of sympathy and snaps at them, "Don't drop crumbs! And be sure you share them fairly. Who knows how long we'll be at sea."

In the doorway she turns around once more and glances again at the two penguins munching away. "Hmm," she says. "I have a funny feeling that I've forgotten something. Something important." She scratches her head and murmurs, "Oh well, it'll come back to me." Then she quickly pulls the door shut behind her.

Immediately, the third penguin hops out of the suitcase and stretches his wings out greedily for the crackers. For a long while, there is nothing to be heard in the deepest depths of the ark except the penguins' quiet crunching.

Down in the ark there is neither day nor night. The light-bulb sways from one side to the other. Everything smells like tar. "Oh," groans the little penguin, "I wish I were drowned at the bottom of the sea." The journey feels like an eternity. The crackers have long since been eaten. The penguins lie on

their backs, listening to the pelting rain and their rumbling tummies.

"Oh," the little penguin moans again, "I wish I were drowned at the bottom of the sea."

"If you say that one more time," the other two penguins tell him, "we'll throw you overboard."

"Good," wails the little penguin. "That way, I'd finally be drowned at the bottom of the sea!" Then he looks at his friends and thinks, *I bet they've long since regretted smuggling me on board. One of us keeps having to hide in that suitcase. The dove's bound to find us out sooner or later. My friends should have just let me drown. That would have been easiest for all of us.*

The other two are thinking, *We should never have started this scam. We should have told the dove that we were three friends and that we weren't going to let one of us drown. We should have said that penguins only come in threesomes, and if God doesn't like it, then he'll have to face a penguin-less future. End of story.*

The little penguin suddenly breaks the silence. "Do you remember what it was like at home?" They all think hard. It was such a long time ago. Everything was always somehow white. They have a vague memory of snow. Glittering ice everywhere. They snuggled together cozily. They always knew what would happen next — namely, nothing. That was so comforting. Will they ever see their home again? The little penguin begins to sing hoarsely:

> *"If you're feeling sad and low,*
> *shut your eyes*
> *and dream of snow*
> *and think about your —"*

The other two penguins squawk longingly,

"home, home, our home, sweet home!"

Their singing gets louder. "Oh, our home!" they blare out. "Oh, home, sweet home!" They suddenly start dancing. "Oh, our home!" Anyone who has watched a penguin dance knows that they caper around, flap their wings together, and wantonly tumble all over one another. Penguins enjoy dancing so much that they forget everything that's going on around them.

That's why they don't notice the dove storming down to the depths of the ship and wrenching the door open.

"What's all the noise about? I just went to bed!" The dove is wearing a nightcap and shouting so loudly that her face has turned beetroot red. If she hadn't immediately started bellowing and had taken a good look around first, she would surely have noticed that not two but three penguins are rooted to the spot before her, poised in mid-dance. One of them even stammers, "We were just having a little dance to remind us of home."

"I've been on my feet for forty days non-stop," the dove blazes. "The two giraffes were seasick and were dangling their necks over the railings; the peacock was so agitated he kept putting his fan up and taking up all the space; and Noah's no help either. He shut himself in his cabin forty days ago and simply refuses to come out. So absolutely everything falls to me — but do you imagine I've had a word of thanks from anyone at all? Not a bit of it." Then she slams the door shut behind her.

As soon as the dove is gone, the three penguins dare to breathe again. "The dove didn't notice there were three of us!"

"The dove needs glasses." The little one giggles — then suddenly stops. The dove's footsteps are approaching once more. "She's coming back!" With one bound, the little penguin leaps into the suitcase and pulls down the lid.

Not a moment too soon. The dove is standing in the doorway. She has her wings on her hips and is looking around. "Were there just three penguins here?"

"Where on earth could a third penguin have come from?" the other two penguins ask, looking at her innocently.

"I'm sure I saw a third penguin just now." The dove looks around suspiciously.

"Well," the two penguins reply, "that kind of thing's quite normal when you've been on your feet for forty days non-stop, and you're in charge of everything, and you never hear a word of thanks, and Noah's no help, and you don't get to lie down even for a minute. In those circumstances, seeing a third penguin is to be expected."

It has been a long while since anyone has spoken so kindly to the dove. All the other animals spend their whole time moaning and groaning at her.

"You're the only ones who understand me," says the dove, her eyes filling with tears. "You can't imagine how it feels. This rain is never going to stop, I've completely lost hope, the ark was a spur-of-the-moment idea, I always thought it would be a journey to happiness, but I'm starting to think we're going to spend the rest of our lives pitching through the darkness on this lumbering crate without getting anywhere. It would be better if we just all drowned —"

The dove lowers her head, covers her eyes with her wings, and starts sobbing quietly. The two penguins wonder how to get rid of her as quickly as possible without hurting her feelings. They waddle to the door, open it wide, and call, "Goodbye!"

But the dove keeps on sobbing softly.

A voice suddenly breaks the silence. It plainly comes from the suitcase. "Couldn't you have got rid of that stupid dove a bit sooner? I'm starting to run out of air!"

"What was that?" asks the dove.

The two penguins pretend to listen carefully. "We didn't hear anything."

"It came from the suitcase," replies the dove.

The penguins quickly shake their heads.

"I thought that suitcase looked fishy right from the start." The dove taps the lid with the tip of her wing. "Open up!"

The penguins don't move a muscle.

"I want to know what's in there."

"God," calls the little penguin from inside the suitcase.

The dove jumps. "Pardon?"

There is the sound of someone clearing his throat. Then the little penguin speaks again, in a deeper voice this time. "You heard me."

"I don't believe it," laughs the dove.

"You don't believe in God?" The voice sounds threatening this time.

"Yes, I do, but —"

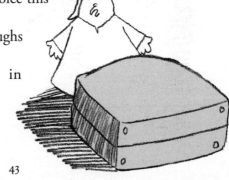

"Well, then," booms the voice.

"But I do find it hard to believe," replies the dove, "that God's in this suitcase."

"Why? God is everywhere."

The dove looks quizzically at the two penguins. They are both nodding their heads.

"Then prove it," says the dove slyly.

"You have to believe in me without demanding proof."

"That's a lot to ask."

"I know, but that's the funny thing about it," says the voice in the suitcase. "Otherwise, it would be too easy. It's not called 'believing in God' for nothing."

The dove thinks for a while before finally saying, "You know what I think?" Then, without waiting for an answer, she carries on. "This is a hoax. I'm simply going to open that case. Then we'll see."

"If you like," says the voice. "But you'll go blind."

"Blind?"

"Anyone who looks at God goes blind. If you're dead set on going blind, then all you have to do is open this suitcase. But be careful; the left buckle's a bit stiff."

The dove looks uncertainly at the two penguins. The first one is wondering if it is true that looking at God makes you go blind, while the second one is desperately hoping that an all-seeing God can see into everything except the depths of the ark.

After a while, the voice continues. "Are you hesitating? That's very sensible of you. Apart from anything else, it would be a terrible shame if a beautiful white dove like you were to lose her sight."

"How do you know I'm a beautiful white dove?"

"Well, because I made you myself. After I'd created the other animals, I said to myself, 'And last of all I want to make a creature that surpasses all the others; a creature in my own image.' And thus I created a white dove."

The dove flutters her wings excitedly. "I'm starting to believe that God really is in that suitcase." Then she throws herself onto the floor in front of the suitcase and cries, "I'm sorry for not believing you."

"It's forgiven and forgotten."

"I never imagined you'd be so understanding."

"Most people have quite the wrong impression of me, sadly."

The dove creeps even closer to the suitcase. "To be honest, I was a bit angry with you."

"It's fine. I can cope with that. It's hard to be angry with someone who doesn't mean anything to you. If you're angry with me, then I must matter to you."

The dove is speechless. The two penguins exchange astonished looks. Where on earth has the little penguin got all this from?

The voice comes from the suitcase again. "Would you like to tell me why you were angry with me?"

The voice still sounds friendly, but the dove has a feeling that her answer is going to matter. Is this a trap? She thinks for a moment, then bursts out, "This flood is a catastrophe!"

The voice in the suitcase replies calmly, "To be honest, I'm not particularly proud of this flood. I might have…"

"Go on," the dove says softly.

"I might have overreacted slightly."

"Overreacted?!"

Even the two penguins look baffled.

"I made a mistake," growls the suitcase.

The two penguins glance at one another, then grab the dove under her wings and escort her to the door. "God's a bit tired."

"Let me go! It's so exciting — I never imagined it would be so good to talk to God in person."

"The pleasure can be yours any time you like," comes the voice from the case. "I am always there for you, wherever you are."

"I'll never doubt you again, and I'm going to tell everyone how marvellous you are, and I guarantee" — the dove stretches her right wing up like a spear — "that in no time at all, everyone will love you as much as I do."

"No need," says the voice good-naturedly. "Everyone has to decide on their own whether they love me or not. Love only means something when it's freely given."

The dove is completely beside herself. She throws her entire body at the suitcase and flings her arms around it. "I've always loved you, but now I love you even more. You're even better than I thought."

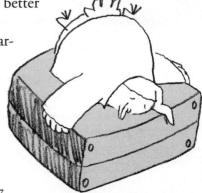

Touched and rather embarrassed, the two penguins turn away as the dove smothers the suitcase with kisses. "But there must be something you want? Tell me — I'll do anything you ask."

"I'd like a cheesecake."

The dove leaps off the suitcase. "A what?"

"A cheesecake."

The three of them stare at the suitcase. There is a long silence. "Maybe we should call it a day for now," the two penguins say cautiously. "It sounds to us as if God is getting a bit tired. This massive flood has completely exhausted him."

"In that case," says the dove, her eyes narrowing to become little slits, "he's all the more deserving of a cheesecake."

A cheer comes from inside the suitcase. "This dove is definitely going to heaven!"

"But," says the dove in honeyed tones, "wouldn't you prefer something a bit more substantial after this exhausting flood?"

"A cheesecake would be fine."

"With a nice brown crust?" cooes the dove.

An enthusiastic gurgle comes from inside the suitcase.

"With lots of raisins?"

"No, the fewer the better."

"And a couple of little colourful umbrellas on top?" pipes the dove.

"I'll never forget what you've done for me!" whoops the little penguin in the suitcase. He has screwed his eyes up in delight and clenched his little wings into fists — and so he doesn't notice the dove slowly opening the lid as he carries on chattering away excitedly, "I have an incredibly good memory, you see, and I'm seriously wondering whether I shouldn't turn you into one of my representatives on earth, and —" Only now does he notice that his voice no longer sounds deep and hollow. He opens his eyes. Before him stands the white dove, with her wings folded in front of her chest.

"I don't know God personally," growls the dove, "but I know one thing for sure: that's not God."

The little penguin clears his throat. "You can't be so certain."

"God isn't a penguin!" the dove bellows at him.

The other two penguins try in vain to convince her that God can take on whatever form he likes, but the dove isn't listening. She is flailing her wings in agitation, losing a couple of feathers in the process, and declaring that she wasn't fooled for a single second, and that the penguins ought to be ashamed of themselves, and that she unfortunately has no choice but to report their deeply distasteful behaviour to Noah himself, and that she knows for a fact that they will be severely punished.

In the doorway, the dove turns around again. "Penguins like you will get very short shrift here on the ark." Then she quietly shuts the door behind her.

"Cheesecake, of all things," groan the other two penguins.

"I couldn't think of anything else," the little one says sheepishly.

"The dove ought to have realized then that you weren't God," says the first penguin.

"I realized it even a bit before," the second one adds.

"Realized what?"

"That you weren't God."

"Did you actually think," the little penguin asks incredulously, "that God was in the suitcase?"

"Yes, for a minute. You really were very convincing."

The little penguin blushes with pride. "I didn't even have to think about it. The words just popped into my head."

At that point, the third penguin completely loses his cool. "Are you two crazy? God would never admit to making a mistake. You pretended to be God, and that's, that's" — his voice cracks — "there must be a word for it, but I don't know what it is. Or maybe there isn't even a word for it, because nobody's ever committed such a terrible crime before. We'll all be severely punished. I can already see a huge fist hovering above us."

"Maybe God's completely different from how we imagine him," the other two murmur. "He doesn't bear grudges, that's for sure." But they aren't completely convinced. They bow their heads and wait for the threatened short shrift.

The penguins wait and wonder about their punishment. They aren't sure what "short shrift" amounts to, but it doesn't exactly sound good. They soon lose track of whether they have been awaiting their punishment for a minute, a day, or an entire week. They seem to be waiting for ever. "Maybe the punishment will never come," the penguins muse, "and waiting for the punishment is the punishment."

There is a sudden violent jolt. The floor begins to heave. The penguins clatter into one another. Screams come from all directions. Bears growling, sheep baaing, pigs grunting, elephants trumpeting, geese cackling, monkeys chattering, goats bleating, horses neighing, dogs barking, roosters

crowing, frogs croaking, chickens clucking, owls screeching, snakes hissing, hippos belching, deer saying nothing, cows mooing, wolves howling, cats meowing — in short, a deafening noise.

At the same time, there is non-stop stamping and a scraping of countless feet. But almost imperceptibly the animals' voices become fainter and fainter, and the stamping and scraping, too, gradually fade into the distance. After a while the penguins can't hear anything at all. They listen carefully. They can't hear water lapping against the hull. Even the lightbulb hangs motionless from the ceiling.

One of the penguins breaks the silence. "I don't know why, but I'm hungry for a cheesecake all of a sudden." At that moment someone flings the door open.

The white dove is standing in the doorway. She has something in her beak and says, "Thi i a olli bra."

"I beg your pardon?"

"Thii ii a ollii braa," the dove repeats irritably, although the penguins still haven't understood a single word.

"This is an olive branch, you nincompoops," says the dove, once she has removed the branch from her beak. "It stopped raining, and Noah said, 'Off you go, fly around and see if you can spot land anywhere.' I eventually found this olive branch. The flood is over. The water's gone back down. The earth's dry again. What are you waiting for? You can go back onto dry land. All the animals are getting off. As usual, you're last. Even the tortoises are faster than you. Get a move on. Stop dawdling. All the animals have to leave the ark two by two."

The three penguins hold one another's wings tightly. "But we can't leave two by two. There are three of us."

The dove groans in despair. Penguins cause nothing but trouble.

"So where's the second dove then?" the little penguin asks.

The dove scratches her head. "What second — ?"

"If all the animals have to leave the ark two by two," the little penguin continues — but the dove opens her beak and squawks, "I've got it, at last! The whole time, I've had this funny feeling that I'd forgotten something. A partner! I've forgotten to bring the second dove on board." Sobbing loudly, she slides to the floor and covers her face with her wings. "I thought about all the other animals, but I forgot about bringing my own partner. How can I face Noah without a second dove? I could tear all my feathers out! What on earth am I going to do?"

The little penguin thinks for a moment. Then he says, "We're a dove short, but we've got one penguin too many on board."

The others look at him uncomprehendingly.

"Don't you see?" he says, smiling.

"Yes, I see," the first penguin says.

"Me too," the second one quickly adds.

The dove wipes her eyes. "Then presumably you can explain it to me."

"I'm afraid not," the first penguin whispers to her.

The second one shakes his head. "I was just pretending to understand too."

The little penguin calls them all to order by clapping his wings loudly. "Listen. It's simple. Nobody will notice. All we need is —"

Then he lowers his voice and tells the others his plan. The birds put their heads together and whisper excitedly. At length, even the dove understands the plan. "It's risky," she says, "but Noah's an old man. And his eyesight's not much good either. It might work."

And soon there they are: two penguins standing by the door to the ark, holding one another's wings very tightly and squinting. After so many days in the ark, they need to get used to daylight once more. The sun is shining. The sky is a radiant blue. Birds are tweeting somewhere. All that is left of the water is a few glistening puddles. The two penguins waddle cautiously down the steps of the gangway. When they finally have dry land beneath their feet once more, they hear a deep voice. "Welcome to the new world — but please take your shoes off."

In front of them is an old man with a long white beard. He is leaning on a stick and looking at the two penguins through his thick glasses.

"We're not wearing shoes," reply the penguins.

"But you're leaving a black trail behind you." The old man points his stick at the gangway steps. The penguins turn around. The steps are dotted with black footprints.

"Oh, that's just tar," say the two penguins. "It'll wash off."

"I hope you're the last ones," says the old man.

"There are two more to come." The two penguins point their wings at the gangway. At the entrance to the ark are two doves. Two?

Yes. Two doves. One is plump and white and has forced herself into a black tailcoat that is quite tight under her wings. A black top hat is perched crookedly on her head.

The second dove is a head taller, has a slightly fishy smell, and is swathed from head to toe in an opaque white veil. The veiled dove stumbles awkwardly down the gangway steps as the top-hatted dove anxiously tries to avoid the old man's penetrating gaze.

"These two doves met on board," the penguins explain. "It was love at first sight. They could barely keep their wings off one another, so we married them just to be on the safe side."

"One of them is much bigger than the other," the old man says suspiciously.

"That's completely normal," the penguins reassure him. "Female doves are always a head taller than male ones."

Once the couple is safely on dry land, the two penguins hurry them out of sight of the old man, for the bride has a distinctly fishy smell.

"Thanks for the tickets," they call over their shoulders. "We'll have some great memories of our journey. The catering was so varied, and the entertainment was top-notch."

The little band of birds has almost rounded the first corner when the little penguin turns back once more. He feels as if he hasn't had enough of a chance to speak. And so he opens his beak and says in a surprisingly deep voice, "I don't think I've ever had such a good time as I've had on Noah's ark."

"Just one moment!" The old man raises his stick.

The birds hold their breath. Nobody dares to look around. They are done for. The plump dove removes her top hat, takes a last look at the penguins, then patters slowly across to the old man. She is going to be in huge trouble. She has done everything wrong right from the start. She didn't summon the right animals to the ark; she spent her whole time yelling at them; she smuggled forbidden provisions on board; she played cards with the rattlesnakes; she even dozed off briefly during the long journey. Once land was in sight, all she found was a pitiful olive branch — not to mention having forgotten her partner in the first place. To top it all, she disguised a penguin as a dove and — even worse — she assumed that Noah would fall for it. Stricken with guilt, the dove lowers her head.

"I haven't had chance to thank you yet," she hears the old man saying. "I know what you have accomplished. The ant found her partner again. The giraffes are fit and healthy once more. The antelopes slept peacefully next to the lions. Not a single animal on the ark has eaten another one. That's little short of miraculous. And it's all thanks to your tireless efforts."

The dove looks gratefully at Noah. Her eyes are brimming with tears. She feels like hugging the old man.

"But why did you bring these penguins on board?" Noah asks. "Penguins can swim."

For a moment, the dove is so utterly silent that they can almost hear her mind whirring. "You can — what?" she screeches.

"It's true," say the penguins, slapping their foreheads with their wings. "Yes, we can swim."

They quite forgot this in all the commotion. But it had been the end of the world. That's bound to make you forget such trivial things.

"We're brilliant swimmers," the bride says in his deep voice.

The other two penguins, however, give him a shove. "You can't swim — you're a dove."

"Ah, yes," the bride whispers. "I'm not a penguin."

The old man shakes his head. "Well, it was nice meeting you."

"I hope we meet again soon," the two penguins call.

"At the next flood, if not before," adds the bride, giggling exuberantly.

58

"Oh no," groans the dove.

"There never will be another flood," says the old man, sounding almost disappointed. "God has sworn it."

"But we can't swear that we'll always be good," the bride pipes up.

"Though we will try our best," the other two penguins quickly add, giving the bride a kick.

"God knows that nobody can change," the old man says, watching the penguins kick one another. "Humans and animals alike. There will always be strife, but God has promised never to punish anyone again."

"How do you know?" the penguins say, staring wide-eyed at the man. "You're God, aren't you?"

The old man strokes his long white beard and smiles. Before he can reply, though, the plump dove starts to laugh out loud. "That's Noah, you nincompoops!" She laughs so hard that she tumbles over backward and lands on the ground. She lies there with her wings and legs outstretched, giggles three times more, and then suddenly starts to snore. This is hardly surprising. The dove has been on her feet for forty days, and as soon as she is able to lie down at long last, she falls into a deep sleep.

"I'm not God," says Noah, flattered.

"But you're just how we imagined God to be," the penguins reply. "An old man with a long white beard."

"That's what lots of people think," says Noah. "But God isn't a man."

"So is he a woman?"

"No!" Noah's glasses glint.

"I see," says the first penguin. "So God's more a kind of thing."

"Like a toaster?" the veiled penguin asks.

"You can imagine God to be any way you like," says Noah, "but he's everywhere. In every human, in every animal, in every plant and —"

"Just a moment," the first penguin interrupts him. "So does God admit that this flood was a mistake?"

Noah points his stick toward the horizon. There they can see a rainbow. "This rainbow is a sign from God that the rain will never again blot out the sun for such an immensely long time."

"That's a noble gesture," the penguins say, wide-eyed. If they had been wearing hats, they would have removed them.

"I think it's very decent of God to admit that he made a mistake," says the little penguin.

The penguins stare at the rainbow until they start to feel dizzy. Noah has meanwhile gone back up the gangway and disappeared into his ark.

The disguised penguin glances at the snoring dove. "The poor dear missed the rainbow."

"You can take your disguise off now," the others tell him.

"Actually I quite like myself in this get-up."

The others give him a severe look. "You're a penguin, not a dove. I hope you're fully aware of that."

The disguised penguin blushes beneath his veil, and kicks the other two. If you kick penguins, they will always kick you back — unless they have promised to be good for ever.

"If we start squabbling, there'll be another flood," the first penguin warns the other two.

"No," the second one replies, "God swore he'd never send a flood again."

"Maybe there's no such thing as God, and it just rained for an unusually long time," muses the disguised penguin.

"If there's no such thing as God, why are we spending so much time talking about him?" the other two ask.

"So we don't feel so alone?"

The other two giggle. "You're just over-tired."

At that moment, something flutters up to them. Something small and yellow that flutters three times around their heads.

"A butterfly!" says the little penguin, hopping up and down.

"Two!" the other two cry, pointing to a second yellow butterfly that is following the first one.

"Do you think it's my butterfly?"

"You'll see if you run after him."

The little penguin waddles along excitedly in pursuit of the two butterflies. "It's my butterfly!" he cheers. "I can tell. His left wing is still a bit crumpled."

The other two penguins wink at one another. Then they look once more at the snoring dove. The disguised penguin suddenly scurries over to her, draws back his veil, and kisses her. Surprised, the dove opens her eyes and returns the kiss.

But when she realizes that she has just kissed a penguin, she shuts her eyes again, embarrassed. Then she puts her wings around the penguin and hugs him tight.

Since that day, the dove and the penguin have been inseparable. Every now and then, some animal comments that it really isn't right; the rattlesnakes in particular are inclined to come along and say that God would never have sanctioned such a union. But the dove and the penguin don't care. For meanwhile they have become very fond of one another.

PUSHKIN CHILDREN'S BOOKS

Just as we all are, children are fascinated by stories. From the earliest age, we love to hear about monsters and heroes, romance and death, disaster and rescue, from every place and time.

We created Pushkin Children's Books to share these tales from different languages and cultures with younger readers, and to open the door to the wide, colourful worlds these stories offer.

From picture books and adventure stories to fairy tales and classics, and from fifty-year-old bestsellers to current huge successes abroad, the books on the Pushkin Children's list reflect the very best stories from around the world, for our most discerning readers of all: children.